THE NATIONAL P

The National Poetry Series was established in 1978
to ensure the publication of five poetry books
annually through participating publishers.
Publication is funded by the late James A. Michener,
the Copernicus Society of America, Edward J. Piszek,
the Lannan Foundation, the National Endowment
for the Arts, and the Tiny Tiger Foundation.

2003 COMPETITION WINNERS

Raymond McDaniel of Ann Arbor, Michigan
Murder (a violet), chosen by Anselm Hollo

Stephen Cramer of Astoria, New York
Shiva's Drum, chosen by Grace Schulman,
University of Illinois Press

Andrew Feld of Eugene, Oregon
Citizen, chosen by Ellen Bryant Voigt,
HarperCollins Publishers

John Spaulding of Phoenix, Arizona
The White Train: Poems from Photographs, chosen by Henry Taylor,
Louisiana State University Press

Mark Yakich of Oakland, California
Unrelated Individuals Forming a Group Waiting to Cross,
chosen by James Galvin,
Penguin Books

Murder

[A VIOLET]

RAYMOND McDANIEL

The National Poetry Series
selected by Anselm Hollo

COFFEE HOUSE PRESS

Minneapolis

Coffee House Press books are available to the trade through our primary distributor, Consortium Book Sales & Distribution, 1045 Westgate Drive, Saint Paul, MN 55114. For personal orders, catalogs, or other information, write to: Coffee House Press, 27 North Fourth Street, Suite 400, Minneapolis, MN 55401.

Coffee House Press is a nonprofit literary publishing house. Support from private foundations, corporate giving programs, government programs, and generous individuals help make the publication of our books possible. We gratefully acknowledge their support in detail in the back of this book.

LIBRARY OF CONGRESS CATALOGING-IN-PUBLICATION DATA
McDaniel, Raymond

McDaniel, Raymond, 1969–
Murder (a violet) /Raymond McDaniel.
p. cm.
Includes bibliographical references.
ISBN 1-56689-165-5 (alk. paper)
I. Title.
PS3613.C3868M87 2004
811'.6--DC22
2004012791

FIRST EDITION | FIRST PRINTING
1 3 5 7 9 8 6 4 2
Printed in the United States

The author would like to thank the editors of the following magazines in which elements of *Murder* appear: *Spinning Jenny, American Letters & Commentary, failbetter, Bombay Gin,* and *Southeast Review.*

Sanford
Bette Rae
Sherron
Rex
& Michallene

without whom, nothing

Murder is constructed according to the principle of holographic memory, which dictates that every fragment of an image, no matter how small, contains all the information relevant to that image, every detail necessary to achieve its perfect reconstruction. Therefore, these fragments describe by accretion, rather than by sequence. *Murder* is meant to be unbound, to be read in infinitely different orders. Readers should feel free to make use of the lack of pagination herein to sort the mosaic in whatever ways they find evocative.

Imagine an epic from which a minor character walks away.
    Epic-adjacent.

This soldier appears outside the walls of a cloister as the sisters sleep.

to what shape can steel already bent be shorn?

mosaic of pearl and glass and steel

the vines plucked from abbey stones

vines of violet grapes their strength between stones

as one grows into the other, stone and sap indistinguishable

The assassin escapes her academy. Escapes murder, her trade.
    The janissaries who raised and taught her.

To determine if she can be else, be other, than the violence
    that inheres in her reflex and imagination.

The penitent vaults the wall.

she whom we called indigo she whom we called violet:

The killer.

contents

janissaries make their own salvific claim	*report from the gilt nature of the feral*
janissaries invoke the intimacies of the assassins	*prismatica*
soldiers claim and abandon their bodies	*straddle*
the penitent notes a proximity of that which she is given to love	*pre-orchestral*
the penitent details an aspect of her training	*instruction for posture*
the assassin commits a murder	*first spring*
sisters dispute their own loyalties	*alleged*
the penitent speaks to the sisters' mind	*issuance*
the abbess addresses her sisters	*"there are no mirrors here"*
the penitent recalls old labors and their remedy	*dirty*
sisters press their arguments against the penitent	*panopticon*
the penitent considers the comforts of the janissaries	*later known as*
sisters characterize the contingency of their dilemma	*lapse*
sisters consider the boon of the penitent's labors	*the nursery*
janissaries call the terms of work	*etiquette for exit*
a sister queries the penitent	*"what do you carry with you?"*
world contingent on the murderer's trade is glimpsed	*cold forge*
the assassin has a dialogue with a peer	*conversant*
the penitent admits an affection	*fireworks*
the penitent describes her pleasures as an assassin	*sugar*
the abbess addresses her sisters	*folly*
impossibility of the penitent's punishment is proven	*godless*
sisters of the abbey express their fears	*sovereign sentiments*
possibility of redemption is redefined	*origin of abscess*
garden is subject to nightfall	*seed*
sisters resolve an argument	*fidelity*
a sister declares the minimum	*unstung*
the assassin's appearance at the abbey is re-told	*tint indigo*
warning for abbey and without	*hex after tempest*
essay is	*endeavor*

Murder

[A VIOLET]

of no known name or speech

cannot recall or be recalled

what to do about lilac

watch shade   in slips the penitent

set to say no false thing

speak only with her hands

so list

lilac
indigo
violet

& vague

(here no one ever asks her what she is thinking)

as while sleeping upside down moons open

as during love the weight liquefaction and slide

as if trees reach leaves all oxygen manifest

penitent to what the courtyard opens

murderer to penitent

to stay

application of ocean to sleep
did not arrest her —

murmur and perpetual fall

in this she could sleep

tall woman striding through the wave

but after years her first departure
a return to forest essence in unmemory

she could not sleep without it
the churn and wind's lick at the salt

so remained awake through murder and annunciation
and after

cleaning her hands and her hair
black ink awash in river water

awake for her first meal hungry as if ocean-labored

slip of leaves and boiling river water

every time I drink I will have this to recall

doom

returned to the academy and the water yard

the sound

discussion of colossi migrating into sand

erosion words whispering beneath the door

It does not matter if I do not know so long as someone does

said the word a thousand times
and wondered why the word was better than the world

said her name indigo to sheets taut to windowpanes
to academy chambers and ideal

to apprentice powers and janissaries
to lover malefactor and children

said indigo to answer for crime and request

indigo to wild pigs and antlered hart
polychrome fish and walls like milk
on a boil delayed to a scale planetary

said indigo to dance as divination
to craven craft and lathe and tool

said her name a thousand times and not knowing
who was thereby named

to her reflection indigo abandoned plot and peer

having said, having insufficient, having walked away

slipknot

disappearance as prior

when they seek she is gone
the way the twine's endings approach
as if separate strands and by marriage
make themselves solitary

self-regard that splits

simple selves regard

now untie   now unbind

then small mouthfuls of snow

her hands shadow over the ice

feast that is drown

unknown and no witness

considered as limestone and shell

a spray of shells arrayed along the ear

music tuned to the head's location just dreaming

with foliage to tend as labor

all creeping vines agree no one knows what is inside a ringing bell

thus the penitent maintains privacy

legitimate as aural well and the embrace of lover yet addressed

for this speech her hands unneeded

carols and carillons like that snow

violet   yes

no means to deny it

precedent for retreat as peace these walls both open and home

(this habitation is also epistle)

having adopted the motion of a wave

some nights will take thread to sail or unknot nets

or examine the silver jackets of fish in their element

swimming naked as one muscle folded to spasm and flank

she has stepped to fall from stern one rope ringing her ankle

to tug in tide and wake the schools split by her body

silver sheets and the wet warped moon

water defining her every lack

medium to which she cannot admit breath

persistent palms on her chest and ribs

her lips unable to part or whisper or petition:

wave under wave each speech that says *let us in*

the peace of god does not desire excuses

does not want to occupy her sentiments:

the first moment through the door from snow to mid-axis

collision of birdcall all florid
and *elsewhere*

carnal transfer of snow to salt

(walk down to that city and kill all who speak ill of me)

do you wish back the peace of god?

the first dead body is just weight

awful mass
without the idiot spirit

lower your head the hood for blessing

ambitus rex

once to prove the world round
tied a string about her ankle

and walked that world

dwindle around the rope tide
knot of the needle sunk to the core

only to discover some places
prohibit destination

certain walls rule
and to climb them is abdication
of weariness and map

she who would rest in this garden
must first enter it

so formal

then severance in service to the cloister

still point beaded on the surface
of the spinning world

once to prove the world round
abandoned it

every hour of an absence
is liberty not loss

then one stone after another

a well

seasons, seed:

how it is done or near enough

the abbess

she has a story surely
each caregiver each mortal law
in the satellites and rings

every child encircled

do not underestimate the value
of salvation that appears from nowhere

and as for the abbey:

built before you were born

what this string can accommodate   all these letters
meant to be various

but no precept for murder no genius to admire or unseat

guilt sufficient

(note also the vessels' opened blood its slip from violet to red)

all harbor is piracy too

maker

knife into the apple   droplets of water beaded on its flesh

knife sheer of the seeds

the seeds shine against the nail of the thumb

prized loose the seed between callus and forefinger

two fingers forked in soil   the soil beaded on the flesh of the palm

the sour seed in its soil bed

twist and rise   the tree   the fruit

harvest shade glisten to purple the red of the fruit

taut to limb   branch bowing down

if you do not pluck the fruit it will fall

open   and eat

indigo violet & vague
shade for intrigue and evening gown

your garments are invitation to obscure

but provocation still that pitch black
its succor and temptation its tourney

I cannot recall if sanction is curse or benediction

or the way gray becomes the pretense badge of moderation

in truth each color chosen
selections for stealth and accommodation of stain

mostly it was human shades and labor best left
to twilight hours

not to say she looked poorly:

(slip-shades encroach last seconds before recognition)

the reverse

because privileged and gifted
lazy also the apprentice janissary
wanders windows

neither responsible for the instruction of youth
nor youthful herself

apprentice reports to the afternoon

special sunlights of the academy world
and the jade bowl at whose lips she sits

her advantage over dust falling down
treaties of light seeming safe enough and seen

apprentice choice

and impossible to make or refuse

(which would have been to refuse imperfect blindness
knowing that to do so would require forfeiture of expanse
in favor of far away)

whistle along, envy

jade, verdure, fern and lucent
once upon a time

girl crouching there in the branches so that to sit
is to seem hung in the canopy's green sleeves

waiting loose for appropriation of forest floor or birds foreign
to these skies

her hood hung over her head ashen owl and indigo the killer blinks
as if in deliberation

hunter turned and coiled like wire strung between branches

the meat of trees grows ever-outward and hides their hearts

which, if drunken from, will make the world seem as slow
as sunlight sinking down to the heart's meat

at which time the tree will have become hollow

subject to echo and invasion

with the presence of a fine-enough string

a tune to play upon it

allow

refuse the soup she brings us

because her pulse is better primed for harvest
her skin accommodating of steam

how can we tell gift from inclination
what special skill she offers in her effort to achieve soil
that would nourish us

what salt absolves the root and its white matter
from our having dug it up
of all these knives are there any unfit for flesh

what would our refusal deny but her absolution

air parade   beetles of black abalone on strings

string's end fixed to the fingertip

each child and her signature insect swept in current and surf-wind

gossamer thread and daub of glue the wings furious engine

and the children scrawling their letters in the sand

festival of no occasion

shore-time and water-line at the yard of the ocean the academy's gate

this then in the absence of any known day of birth or parent

words scratched in glassine dust and limestone and calcium remains

words of the insects hum in the salt and air

the older carry the younger to their sparse beds

fold them in their arms and sleep

scorpion

continent's face turned from the sun
posture rotation to her nighttime hours

show me

and indigo the killer steps barefoot and backwards to the abbey wall
walks one foot behind the other
counters corners and breech

four-cornered fortification around the abbess

whose gaze never slips from indigo incapable of misstep or pause
lifting her foot from the scorpion unseen yet spared

(proffer poison
onyx armament and arch)

it is very beautiful

the penitent nods

hastens her heel to the scorpion's body:

beautiful

Once when I was a child I played in an empty barrel
the satisfaction

not the filth or that it was forbidden
but the sensation

of scampering along the walls of the barrel —
knowing my weight

would roll the barrel over as I climbed —
that to feel

as if I were scaling the interior wall would last
only so long

as I stopped short, lest the barrel tumble with my weight —
I mention this because

she keeps dreaming of a cliff so high and so sheer
that to scale it

she must eat into the rock with her fingers —
but in the dream

the higher she climbs the more manageable the angle
becomes, until the cliff

is flat, until she could stand upright and walk it clean —
yet as she walks

the wall continues to rotate, until the stone is heaven
bearing down

and her back is to the upended vault of the moon.
In the dream she never

falls, but just continues upward, until up is even,
up is down and

then up again, sky slowly spun empty and filled.
I am trying to tell you something

about this woman — who has asked me to explain
how, if the world

is on a wheel, she can ever learn
to fall.

appearing initially by twos or threes
to seduce with service or satin

janissaries of the academy appear

as amber as heat leonine
from alien climates through which
the plainly simple simply step:

to the academy and companionship

east of warp wave and burgundy ocean

west of cloud wall artificed
and engineered into pillar and fortification

wall as daily lesson and martial memory

embedded as graduate and assassin

so that this along with other worlds entire
becomes *what I did before I came here*

finger catalogue of everything unwanted
one to ten and then the rotation over
digits infinite in enumeration
that which we despise as explicit

sweat as body's sleeve still sufficient
same for saltwater that brine in which her countenance was cured

sleeve baked to the finest sugar her skin
the last gesture before sleep a palm opened

the assassin collected colors from advent to wintertide
floral sliver bloodied with light
and the green of chameleons at rest
yellow light sunk to the cells of ancient trees

I would like this to be my skin
no, this

discard as she chooses

the trail of husks abandoned

seasons change   *why don't we*

of impact damage or cut
the first lesson of the academy is harm and remedy
bone returned to rods wrapped in scarlet ribbon
the bruise left to airs and the ice between assignations

the action of her unwrapping her garments
peeling the cloth from around her skull
and tightening it to a knot above her knee
so that the trickle dwindles —

what her actions lack is haste

but bones stitch as does all flesh

stitch in paces regardless of what is done to stop them
how many skins are struck
or what is pierced or where

solution for abscess

she reverts and therefore worsens:

washing hands in alcohol evaporation
as if skin could know clarity

solution for abscess is sacrifice
including nightdress and pine boards
each detail sign that lattice is mnemonic

I felt punished
for things I hadn't yet done and knew
my exhaustion and not my bravery
would redeem me

confession trumps penance
welcome acquiescence and mirror-hall

gave it up surrendered superlative

gave it up but what didn't I

not what I used to be:

true and not true, true as diminishment but not regret

kissed a girl between towns each town civil
though the roads between the unclaimed so unseen
all orders are undone

cradled the boy under the dogwood tree those leaves
each a page waiting for eclipse light falling away
his hair stiff and his lips gone waxen

the roads were supposed between the worlds
and then the worlds merely came to interrupt the roads

sometimes the farm would collapse in a sigh of ash
sometimes the boy stumbled in his shoes from door to porch

details, I came to realize, do not much matter

then why his boy-thick fingers and the scent of jade
drained to blooms

this, too

entered west departed east don't know where that road goes perhaps she is beast as rhythm is a beast —

the sound archived in the jaw, the tendon stitched there,
where the strongest silence obtains

do we not require the sequestered to lock their tongues in boxes of bone
until such time as their will is fit

if you cannot tell between what has been done
and what we do

thumb and forefinger cradling the jaw

hand cradled to address the jaw

finger and thumb on the binding knots

speak now   praise the low sounds   the detonation

I will give no name to the sister whose only error
was the compassion

that by our own fault divided us, but she was
young and still subject

to the beauty this vocation denies — I am certain
she saw in the penitent

a love with which she was unable to adorn
herself — we knew

she watched her in the gardens, watched her
moving stones

and splitting dead trees and bringing plants
from promise

to tendril and finally fruit. Never spoke to her
during that time,

as it was unknown to whom she would speak
or when, with what language

she would address or ever, though her tongue
was always tender

in speech, mild to ears accustomed to silence.
On one night

this sister, unable to sleep herself, stole to the gardens
to see her sleeping —

it was known that the penitent preferred to rest without
shift or sheet or pillow —

our sister seeing this crept to her side to gaze
at that face and body.

I cannot say that she alone was moved by this.
But our sister

reached out to stroke that skin and found herself
suspended. The hand

around her neck, by her own report, was neither
forgiving nor harsh.

She held her like that for long moments —
our sister speechless

but unstung, finally crying out when released.
We know this woman

cannot stay here. But I will tell you
that it was not one

of us seen at the side of our sister
that night, seen

beside her, despite the trespass she had made,
singing in unknown syllables

the sound of comfort. We will decide
as we will.

For my part I have seen charity done.

train dogs to their worst and call them courageous
pitch falcons to fields and make their meals our own

we beg profusion of suffering our stitches and sutures sacrifice
think nothing of air slit with feathers
or the feather itself made better than its unshaped best

clean teeth of the dog   pinions preening

houses and uplifted arms and tongue thumbed to whistles
summons to service and service as excruciation

consider the feet of well-loved dogs their journeyman care
pure hunger parlance
coats glisten like the sheen of falcons
to whom we gave sleep

their peace our promise

no murder in hunger for beloved
but distorted to approvals
knots of dogs our viscera unchained
given license and tooth

blame the bird for predation and even murder of the innocent

but not for flying away

neither for flying away

nor for coming back

they birth underground
filthiest of dogs
woman swollen to masquerade
delivered of bitch and cur
each cur given greed

they are dogs

not witnessed numbers not known

skinned or collared or riven or shorn

how many die at birth

academy class graduates are given this

percussion the theme between them
indigo famous for knife and nocturne and botany
her hands slapped to the neck of her partner
swung around and over
her weight drawn tight to the woman's shoulders

catch me

indigo smiling from the arms and hands of her partner
over abyss or cliff the gesture achieved with muscle indistinct from fancy

one knew weather in his head worlds away
one a titan good for damage and fireside counsel
one boy also a golden portal

orphanage laced with murderers and latin vocabulary

noteworthy because she is not guaranteed loyalty despite these lovers
to whom her abdication is lethal

watch, how in the absence of superior structures, they form a circle

striation and sway by which they are conceived

the armor of other in their legs adorned around the back
of this one, that one

without meaning

made as godless they found a worship neither license or rule

this is why my hair (unbound now) is not my hair;
my scent is not my scent
my posture indicates occlusion and theft
our force

in this way we invented both treasure and the place in which it is hidden

arrowhead, fish scale, twine:

memory of motion

pre-orchestral

mass in discord this planned disturbance as implication:

just pressure to drop hand to key and curve as the wrist wills
or touch the leg taut until divot or hillock

breathe in staggers and kiss the gold   order noise

what is meant for love is music not mere instrumentation
but her skin would flutter at the buzz and din of it
selfish sound of mortal drum touched to tool

like loving the flat affect of steel   barely adorned geometric

all line and absent width   ruler and heft

swung to whistles clipped

then the bite in bodies

first a hush and then the sound of washing hands:

afterwards I couldn't listen to music for hours

to sit in a chair that does not exist:
her gravity split from stillness to step-sequence

strike and recoil

dancing with partners who depend on posture

deliquescence water's weight flung
against gravity

flung to clutch or pierce

for years this stand and dance before they put steel in her hand
by which time she stepped into the gesture
more easily than she knew to walk without it

needle and piece of cork
sometimes lightning if the temper's ill

after a while it became hard to tell the difference between the two

first spring

to the accelerated a running man
looks more like a man who is falling

and to extract a core of his colors and manner
is as to pluck a wildflower and drink
milk from its stem

if a man endeavoring to flee has limbs that unfold
like the most febrile of flowers

then the trees themselves
do not seem to move at all
too slow to change or judge what whispers around them

which may explain why she sent the steel through his throat
and saw it as silver stamen

as shine

beheld his blood but believed *orchid*

learned by the world alone to comfort kind and kin
all thoughts lonely later secondary to rest
a hollow free from harm a shelf under which we sleep

fidelity by form and the first fear of danger to those who nestled you

discipline empty to this loyalty unknown

if to remedy her nature is to relieve the girl
or undo her

on what viciousness is built your faith, sister?

would you have us leave the door open to wolves
if we resembled them?

if she is learned, by whom?

swell open, furrows —

her hand the heft of the pole, tip scorched sharp
for digging —

flesh of the root and flesh of the worm and rich

her shoulders opening up to new wings
and the garden unsettled at her bare feet

(woman reaching for green grape light
her loins bunched and full)

grape light, sun light, still shadowed with moons

we would like to speak with you

pole parallel to her shoulders her arms hung
across the sharpened stick

dirt in her lashes and beneath her nails

her back to them, her armature:

I should be destroyed

Perhaps I believe my lies are truth
and this satisfies me —

if it were so then I would know no difference
between what was

and what was false. Please consider
the position

I am given here. You look to me to lead.
To lead

is not my place — we are here not to travel
but to cease the same.

Where would I lead you, then? I am
oldest, only.

My voice contains no greater depth
than yours.

When you look for me in my chambers
am I not there?

Think on why we have no library here,
no pages,

no strings meaningful with knots,
no record writ

in mosaic stones and green glass.
These walls and rooms

were made to fit the garden's need
and we a part

of that garden. Does it then matter
what I believe?

I believe she found her way to this place
without knowing it.

I believe she would have asked sanctuary
from anyone

and perhaps has. I believe we cannot
know if she threatens

until there is harm. Ask yourselves
why she is occasion

to query of me. Did I ask
when you came here?

Did you ask of me? Cast your questions
otherwise.

I have no more labor to offer you.

getting dressed in sweat and stain the paint
particulate

filth the garment of beads sewn from every last thing
in this world

fruit the seal of a dress snug against the skin
each crease marking the joints of good use

washed-down brown of the smile
mud cloak carried in crevasse

just to stand in water and weigh
shuck skin and shave and sleep in sheets clean

as all the troubles we have passed away

panopticon

if there is a home to which she can return
the decision should be made other than by hunger

outside these walls she becomes acute

lessen the succor the sharper she sees

and will not ask forever to have these eyes taken away from her

will she still be able to see in starlight scale and feature
or will she be blind and would that differ
or will she stare at the suffering in series or a single scene forever

beseech thee

these gifts are not ours to withdraw

good at it but not about excuses

rather principles

those few in rooms not stained with sweat
or physics in defiance

whose task is metaphor and placement of simple terms

secret shades from the world's dense heart thick
like a pearl lovely grit compressed to value

just to say the janissary cure was to offer alternate:

there are places where these acts are unperformed
and each option realized in turn

but in each world where you are midwife or carpenter
no room remains

came a moment when she wished for nothing
more than this:

pass herself down some hallway and ask a man

who is she, I don't know her, what's her name

lapse

    see the lattice go opaque
    the stone split a backward clap

    watch water freeze a jar into fragments
    for too complete with water, unladled

    the crack in the wall issues thin and crescent

    had we but drank

    or perhaps her ice to evening all over again

afraid that to love animals was to not know her own teeth
as loving the sea was once imagination
before she came to pluck bubbles from that suit
the sea her second skin

the crush of waters drawn back together and her between

or flight more like falling
loss of direction bought with bones like reeds
organs that release devotion to her claws their iris

the least of these fruits grows no more slowly than I do

one day they will drink the wine pressed from those grapes
bunched then unfurled as her labor

is it sin that bounty is also given to these hands
if the innocent do profit from it

gratitude for power for protection

bliss in callus and shield

these yards her fruits and labors penance with pleasure

drink: *it is my soil, also*

etiquette for exit

janissaries joined at the thought of a tongue
implicit in instruction and aged into alabaster

he and she who extract from these tasks a dignity

and touched the lips and foreheads of the class:

sometimes it will be as simple as folding a garment over your shoulders
or turning down the stairs to the cellar

and sometimes you will have to make infirm all the organs
of those in your wake

of course it is always best to stay unseen
save to each other

and indigo her allies and caste

they practiced

not steel

for I can fashion its equal from prop or broom
though I would regret the loss of this name

not shell

for I can find cousin's design under the leaves of ferns
or in a cloud's stuttering

neither coat nor hood

for these I can take wherever I find them, from bodies if needed,
who need them no longer

not food

for what I eat I find fallen or kill myself

just your colors then

which I inhabit

and your carriage and limbs

tied together at angles and ends

my flesh, for which there is no equivalent

cold forge

some family's pride, this skill

rooms and records devoted to heritage
tapestry permission and seal

license to love the metal
beaten flat so many times the hammer becomes
the domestic —

rhythm to which the children play the doll's dances done for forge —

spark and fold

dishes dropped in rhythm food swallowed
and the sun a plummet then buoy as a hammer falls

metal folded over to hardship

as the smith hands his daughter the edge for sharpening
her rhythm a tide maintained with muscle

beautiful labor

beautiful use

on occasion at the academy's discretion:
a marriage of satellites

to her he was the man whose skin shaded out to pure pitch
unseen under starlight and invisible in corners
known for his folding of faith into deeds done
the castles and arteries of an honored family
for whom he had ossified into the devil

and to him she was quiet violet the killer
best remembered to stare a scene until sight
became sentence indigo also
the one of them with the best balance

task completed and meant to atom away
she said to him *it is good to have allies*

as he brushed sand on his hands to dry them
and said

against whom

fireworks

slip through flora all green gone gray with night
the assassin slides down the hill her fingers fan
leaves as they pass

fireworks fall a delinquent thunder above her
scarlet glistens and flickers on her face

falling into the river laughter warps in bubbles
from her mouth
as ash settles into the current

what do you love about it

fireworks

fire   she laughs   *works*

belonging here girl addition fading in:

the thread on which sugar hangs in a glass pregnant with sweet

saturated and stirred arc tip satisfaction made crystal and brittle

scatter of perfect planes to please the tongue

as many actions are

hips pivot to the cervix cupped rotation as orbit

slow addition of armament to orchestra each brass and reed

and extension of arm to stick or stone or shot

action multiplies to satisfaction stupid as all numbers are

obedient to extra

supplemental to the glass of water the thread evidence alone

of sweet: so much sugar spun to molecules

the taste pleasure despite poison   sugarwater sweet

taste: could you have stopped me? could you? could you?

Yes everything is. Of what comfort is that?
You crave

judgment and I will not give it, yet
I do not think

this will prevent you from pulling it from me.
When these rooms

were twine on the ground and just my desire
I killed

to raise them up —— I killed the worms
in the earth beneath

the stones I desired and I killed the saplings
whose supple limbs

were my allies alone. I made shade with these walls
and murdered all

the blooms that would otherwise have been.
If I plant my rake

in the earth like a rod and damn
what will be achieved

but your conviction? Examine my hands.
Is peace there?

Then if I withdraw I cannot take it away.
You approached

her with what weapons you invented
with your imagination

and yet you still live. Do you deserve this life
that still obtains

within you? Or are you less than her mercy,
less because of it?

I am a fool. You are also fools. This changes
nothing.

She departs this place. I depart this place.
Neither can know

to where the other goes. To you who remain,
my peace.

Recall what we have grown here draws
water and weed

from beneath our walls, and sunlight
from above them.

Our houses stand on what we cannot contain.
What is between

wild and our cultivation is folly. This is no
damnation.

I welcome wilderness, those worlds' farewell.
I said this: my peace.

upon waking will stand at once her hands arced inward above her head
one motion as if poured from the earth

if the stones and thin limbs of spring trees call her abomination
and spit forth shoot, tendril and thorn

god's dart and stone shards

fling at her hammers and quarrels and rain

and at her fall there will be air alone

where once

you can employ no device she will not catch or step from

not because I can   flex and point as she considers her hand

because it knows, cannot forget

obscene that spring still comes to the murderer's world
perfect petals and the water loose in the earth

beckon and bring still obscene she weakens to fragrance and birth

sick like tide all motion revealed as mindless

if the translucence is lovely then let it be damned
as those given to love it

strip these worlds of features and the powers to strip them
see the color prime beneath the skin

you must acknowledge what you've done —

as if waking was indeed known as new

as if the jade cathedral sprung from flowering was not also fatal

heliotropic, which suspends will

see, still reaching, uncurling, even now

is to inhere

interruption of intent whether the will is original or not

the action defeats origin so that one cannot tell

when she began or if she has come to end

abscess is not injury

(for she would heal were healing needed
and burn away those skins were it not)

abscess is the hole in motion that is static

the gone-girl neither foresworn nor fulfilled

violet nocturnal waking to suns and satellites

she who turns but turns to stay

seed

who made these?

black grape and plum

plum-skin under supple in the palm of her hand

black grapes thick in a black bowl

the bluish skin of each dust disrupted with her finger's signature

fruit: texture tight over the pulp

and the seeds thin between her teeth, the taste bitter

burn them for their oil if at night you are ill at ease

black grape and plum

who made

glory

(if knowing the names of plate and fissure compromise
this gesture

then hush

take your peace)

and go

to what shape can steel already bent be shorn

vines plucked from abbey stones

vines of violet grapes their strength between stones

as one grows into the other through stone and sap indistinguishable

she whom we called indigo she whom we called violet

seen sometimes the hue of assassins
or girls who are very shy

found inside the lip (of conch & sometimes man)

never dawn but planetary

those flowering plants given more to white

and between

for assassins then: *who knows what they do*
and in recollection her guess mostly fashions

long vertical crease and gull-colored
known only in pieces
as if the skill was known as lovers
her hand the slip cascade of haste

who knows what they do

why should this girl in peculiar be comfort to me

all ill and irresistible   *it was not resistance that was my desire to achieve:*

violet

hex after tempest

leaderless   came-through-the-window

resist the smile that goes with even the most severe of sentences

she moved around our gardens like a flutter a handful of stones

something terrible sharp

regard abscess that also opens
affection that tendrils from the mad as gratitude
and these yards' fatal good will

gardens and walls

this embassy of the bamboo

although brief

the affections

by which our home is made

Thank you / Anselm Hollo   Frank Bidart   Samuel Delany
Claudia Rankine   Susan Stewart   Rebecca Wolff   C. D. Wright

Thank you / Christopher Fischbach   Molly Mikolowski
all the avengers at Coffee House Press

sterling / Cara Spindler   Michael Dickman

unfailing / Miss Meghan Cleary   the poet m loncar

peacock and pepper / Nickole Brown

edit and essential / Cheri Hickman

century surgeries / Christine Hume

aeroplane and apiary / Amanda Kelly McDaniel

colophon

Murder (a violet) was designed at Coffee House Press in the warehouse district of downtown Minneapolis. The text is set in Spectrum with page indicators in Galahad.

funder acknowledgment

Coffee House Press is an independent nonprofit literary publisher. Our books are made possible through the generous support of grants and gifts from many foundations, corporate giving programs, individuals, and through state and federal support. Coffee House Press has received support from the Minnesota State Arts Board, through an appropriation by the Minnesota State Legislature and from the National Endowment for the Arts, a federal agency; and from grants from the Elmer and Eleanor Andersen Foundation; the Buuck Family Foundation; the Bush Foundation; the Butler Family Foundation; the Grotto Foundation; the Lerner Family Foundation; the McKnight Foundation; the Outagamie Foundation; the Pacific Foundation; the John and Beverly Rollwagen Foundation; the law firm of Schwegman, Lundberg, Woessner & Kluth, P.A.; St. Paul Companies; Target, Marshall Field's, and Mervyn's with support from the Target Foundation; James R. Thorpe Foundation; West Group; the Woessner Freeman Foundation; and many individual donors.

This activity is made possible in part by a grant from the Minnesota State Arts Board, through an appropriation by the Minnesota State Legislature and a grant from the National Endowment for the Arts.

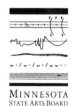

To you and our many readers across the country, we send our thanks for your continuing support.

Good books are brewing at coffeehousepress.org